Text copyright © Jeremy Strong 1998
Illustrations copyright © David Mostyn 1998

First published in 1998

First published in Great Britain in 1998
by Macdonald Young Books
an imprint of Wayland Publishers Ltd
61 Western Road
Hove
East Sussex
BN3 1JD

Find Macdonald Young Books on the internet at
http://www.myb.co.uk

The right of Jeremy Strong to be identified as the author
and of this work and the right of David Mostyn to be
identified as the illustrator of this Work has been
asserted by them in accordance with the
Copyright, Designs and Patents Act 1988.

Designed and Typeset by Backup Creative Services, Dorset DT10 1DB
Printed and bound in Belgium by Proost International Book Production

British Library Cataloguing in Publication Data available

ISBN: 0 7500 2564 6

JEREMY STRONG

Max and the Petnappers

Illustrated by David Mostyn

Chapter One

"How extraordinary!" cried Max's dad,
staring into the pond through his extra-thick
spectacles. "Somebody has kidnapped all
our goldfish. Look at this!" he waved a
scribbled note in front of Max.

WE HAVE YOUR GOLDFISH.
HAND OVER A HUNDRED POUNDS
OR WE'LL DROWN THEM!

"It's the petnappers," Max explained grimly. "We've been talking about them at school. They've been stealing pets from round here and holding them to ransom."

Max's dad shook his head in disbelief. "Some people are very strange…"

Max thought this last remark was a bit much, coming from his dad. Max reckoned he probably had the strangest dad in the world.

Max's dad was an inventor. He had great wavy mounds of hair and thick spectacles that made his eyes bulge like ping-pong balls. He was always inventing something odd, and Max never knew what his dad would do next.

Come to think of it, he never knew what his mum would do next either. She was a surprise too, because she could never quite decide what it was she wanted to be.

Last week she had wanted to be a rock drummer. This week she wanted to be a rock *climber*. She had fixed ropes all over the house, inside and out. Max's mum climbed up the walls, and she climbed up the stairs. When she went to the loo she wore her climber's hat and clipped herself to the wall, just in case she fell off.

Before they had any time to think about the petnappers there was a bleep-beep from the fax machine and a message appeared. Max's mum read it and turned a

shade paler. "Aunt Claribel is coming to stay for a few days."

"My sister?" squeaked Dad, with some alarm.

"Who's Aunt Claribel?" asked Max. "I've never heard of her before." But his parents were already too busy to answer him.

Max's dad handed a fat roll of sticky tape to his wife. "We'd better tape up the windows," he declared. "Do the upstairs first." So Max's mum shinned up the house walls and stuck big crosses of tape on every window.

"Is this a new invention?" asked Max, wondering what was going on.

"Invention!" cried Dad. "Brilliant idea! What we need is a goldfish detector. Now let's see…" and Max's dad went hurrying off to his Inventing Shed before Max could find out why the windows were being taped up. Max was still thinking about them when he was disturbed by an insistent clatter from above, growing louder and louder. Max stared up at the sky, wondering what it was.

Chapter Two

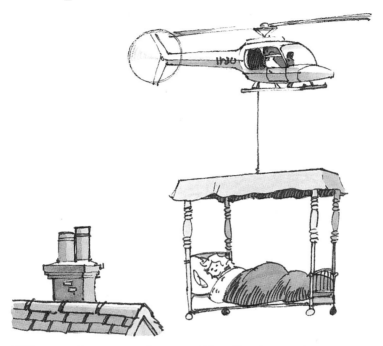

The noise was Aunt Claribel. At least it wasn't Aunt Claribel herself, but it was the noise of her approach.

Claribel arrived by bed – an enormous four-poster – and the bed was attached to a long piece of strong wire, and the wire was attached to a helicopter. The helicopter hovered over the house and Aunt Claribel was slowly lowered into the front garden.

The wire was detached and the helicopter buzzed away, leaving Aunt Claribel lying in bed on the front lawn, fast asleep.

"Claribel!" cried Max's dad, running out to his sister. Aunt Claribel woke with a startled grunt and stared at her brother.

"Bangerboots!" cried Claribel, and she heaved herself from the bed (she was a very large lady) and squashed her brother to her chest in an enormous hug.

"Bangerboots?" Max wrinkled his nose.

"Claribel always called your dad 'Bangerboots'," explained Mum. "Even when he was small his inventions were always exploding." Aunt Claribel stopped trying to suffocate Max's dad and pushed him away.

"I must do my exercises at once," Claribel declared seriously.

"Are you sure?" asked Max's dad, looking very anxious.

"Yes, I must. Stand back everyone…"

Max wondered what Claribel was going to do. Maybe she would do a back flip, or a handstand? But no, Claribel didn't do any of that stuff. Aunt Claribel threw her arms wide. She shut her eyes. She tipped back her head and opened her mouth and…

"La-ah, da-ah, lo-dee do-dee lo-dee do-dee la la la la waaaaaaaaahhhh!!!!!!"

Birds fell out of their nests in alarm. Cats everywhere began to howl in a noisy chorus. Burglar alarms went off up and down the street. Every window in the house rattled and threatened to burst into tiny fragments, and Max suddenly realized what all the tape was for. Obviously his parents were used to this. He took cover behind the settee with his mother.

"What is she doing?"

"Didn't Dad tell you? Your Aunt Claribel is a very famous opera singer. She's just doing her warming-up exercises. Here, put some of this cheese in your ears. I find it sounds a lot better through a bit of cheddar."

Chapter Three

Aunt Claribel was just getting under way with her singing exercises when an ancient green van went burping and bouncing past the house. The van had black tinted windows, so that nobody could see who was inside. Along each side of the van and across the back door were the words:

SNITCH & GRAPPLE
We will do *Anything* (for money)

The van lurched to a halt. A small flap in the roof of the van flipped open and up popped a periscope. It peered this way and that way, until at last it fixed upon Aunt Claribel in Max's front garden, singing her heart out. (Although it sounded more like *all* her insides, not just her heart.) At the other end of the periscope was a pair of very beady eyes, belonging to the squid-like face of Belladonna Snitch.

Belladonna gave a chuckle and turned to her companion, Gretel Grapple. "Do you know what I can see?"

"Ha, ha!" Gretel's laugh sounded more like a duck's than a human's. "No – what is it? Is it a dog? A cat?"

"No, something bigger…"

"Horse, cow, pig, sheep – elephant?"

"A bit like an elephant," admitted Belladonna. "But no - I spy with my little eye Claribel Tinkleton, the famous opera star. What's more, she earns mega bucks."

"Ha ha. She must be rich then," Gretel said.

"Of course she's rich, jelly-brain!" A cunning smile spread across Belladonna's toothy face. "So, what are we going to do then?"

"Have some breakfast?" suggested Gretel hopefully.

"Of course not! Don't you ever think of anything else?"

Gretel looked hurt. "Of course I do," she mumbled. "Sometimes I think of lunch, or tea, or – *ow*! That hurt!"

"It was meant to hurt. Listen carefully. We are going to kidnap Claribel Tinkleton, and then we are going to..."

"...have breakfast?" added Gretel brightly.

"No! We are going to kidnap her and hold her to ransom."

"But I thought we were kidnapping people's pets?"

"That's just chicken-feed," sneered Belladonna. "Listen, if we grab La La Tinkleton we can ransom her for a million pounds and then you can have a thousand breakfasts. What do you think of that for an idea?"

Gretel took another peep through the periscope and listened to the noise from beyond the van. "She will stop singing first, won't she?"

Belladonna Snitch grinned. "Gretel, we are going to be fabulously rich."

"You said that last week," Gretel reminded her partner.

Chapter Four

Max was not sure that he liked having
Aunt Claribel in the house. It was all right
when she wasn't singing, but she hardly
ever stopped. She sang in the bath. She
sang in the toilet. She even sang in the
supermarket. Everyone stared and Max
turned bright red.

"Tra la lah, oranges and apples, put them in the ba-ha-ahsket, with an onion here and tomato soup, a-doopee-doop!" Then everyone in the supermarket burst out clapping and pointing.

"Look! That's Claribel Tinkleton! Quick, get her autograph!"

Max enjoyed being seen with someone famous, even if he didn't like the singing. Besides, Aunt Claribel did look rather splendid.

She wore bright, sweeping dresses that swirled and rustled and flapped about her body like giant tropical plants. Before she went to sleep Claribel would sit on her

bed in the front garden and sing a lullaby to the street, leaving everyone wide awake and their ears ringing. Then she would tuck herself up and quickly slip into a deep slumber. "I always sleep in the open air," she told Max. "It keeps my air passages open and fresh... gives me a purer tone you know."

"Laaaahahah-aahh!"

Max went upstairs to bed and stuffed his head beneath a pillow, but even like that he could still hear Aunt Claribel's operatic snores wafting up from the garden. At last he managed to drift off to sleep.

In the darkest depths of the night a battered green van growled and grumbled to a halt outside Max's house. The flap in the roof opened and up went the periscope. "I don't believe it!" muttered Belladonna. "The silly whale is sleeping in the front garden. This is going to be so easy!"

"A whale?" asked Gretel. "We can't kidnap a whale. It won't fit in the van, and even if it did we'd have to fill it with water and then we'd drown and…"

"It's not a real whale, you pumpkin head! It's Tralala Tinkleton. Listen, this is what we do…"

Inside the house Max stirred. He
needed a visit to the bathroom. He got up,
then stopped and listened. He could hear
weird clanking noises. Max peered out of
the window and his eyes popped. Two
shadowy figures were fixing a chain to
Aunt Claribel's enormous bed. They
carried the chain over the front fence
and out to the road, where they wrapped
it round the tow bar on the back of
their van.

With a volcanic roar the engine erupted
into life. The tyres screeched, sending
clouds of rubbery smoke into the air.
The chain tightened and suddenly:
KHAWWAANNNGGG!!!

Aunt Claribel's bed went lurching across
the grass, crashed through the garden
fence and went zigzagging up the road,
its little castor wheels clattering and
bouncing on the tarmac. Max went racing
downstairs, plunged out through the front
door, and set off after the kidnappers.
He ran like fury and just as the careering
bed reached the corner he managed to
grab the end and haul himself on board,
still in his pyjamas.

Chapter Five

No matter how hard Max shook Aunt
Claribel, she carried on snoring. The van
shot down a narrow road and on to a dark
industrial estate. It screeched to a halt
outside a big garage with roll-up doors.
Max slipped under the bedclothes to hide.

Snitch and Grapple leaped from the van,
unhooked the bed and pushed it into the
garage. They pulled down the door. Now
nobody would know where they were.

"Brilliant!" cried Snitch. "We've done it! Now, all we have to do is tie up the fat whale and gag her. We don't want her yelling for help. Then we'll go into the back room, make a nice cup of tea and write the ransom note."

"Uh? Wha…?" began Aunt Claribel as she was seized by the kidnappers, and then a gag was shoved over her mouth and her hands tied behind her back. The kidnappers left her there, sitting up in bed and looking like a very startled parrot. (A very *large* startled parrot.)

As soon as the kidnappers had gone into the back room, Max crept out of his hiding-place. Aunt Claribel was even more astonished. Max put one finger to his lips. "Sssssh! You've been kidnapped, Auntie, and look where we are! This must be the petnappers' hide-out!"

The garage was full of boxes, crates and glass tanks – and animals. There were dogs, cats, rats, mice, hamsters, fish, several large spiders, a boa constrictor and a haughty looking chameleon.

Most of them had little labels attached to them, with ransom prices. And there, in a bowl, were Dad's goldfish.

"The petnappers are going to ransom you," whispered Max. "They're in the room next door, so keep quiet. Listen, I've got an escape plan." Max quickly removed the gag and began to whisper in Auntie's ear.

Loud voices came from the other room. "They're coming back," hissed Max. "Get ready...!" He hastily crawled beneath the bed and stuffed his fingers into his ears.

The kidnappers came in and Claribel gathered her robes and rose from the bed like some monstrous bird of prey. She spread her arms wide, closed her eyes, tipped back her head and...

"La la la la la la Wooooooooh!"

"Stop! STOP!" yelled Belladonna, staggering back and clutching her head, but Claribel's voice shrieked and echoed round the garage.

"Eeeeeeeeeeee – neee – neee – neeeeeeeeeh!"

Gretel stumbled about, hands clasped to her ears. She fell to her knees, knocking over boxes and setting eighteen cats, dogs and rabbits scrabbling around her.

She crawled across the floor whimpering, while animals jumped on her back, nipped her ankles and tried to burrow up her sleeves. "Stop, stop!"

Max seized his chance. He grabbed Aunt Claribel by the hand, pulled her outside, quickly shut the door and locked it, leaving the sobbing kidnappers covered

in madly clawing animals and hammering to be let out. Claribel delved deep inside her dress, produced a mobile phone and promptly rang the police.

Max and Claribel sang all the way
home as they were towed by a police car.
(The police had to radio base to ask for
ear-plugs.) Max's mum and dad were
very surprised to find Max and Claribel
arriving home at half-past three in the
morning, but they were delighted when
they heard how Max had caught the
petnappers, rescued Aunt Claribel *and*
saved the goldfish.

Max's dad was inspired to go off and invent something straight away, and he was very pleased with the result, and so was everyone else, except Claribel. Max's dad had invented a soundproof box that fitted over her head. It had a visor on the front so that she could see where she was going, but nobody outside the box could hear a sound – not a single note. Dad's invention actually worked! He was so pleased with himself that he went straight back to invent something else.

Moments later there was a loud explosion. The shed door was blown from its hinges and Max's dad went skidding backwards across the garden, clinging to the door as if it were a giant skateboard. It crashed into the fence.

Dad looked across at them and grinned a sooty grin. "Didn't work!" he cried. "But it will next time!" He hurried back inside the smoking shed.

"Bangerboots!" chorused Mum and Aunt Claribel and Max.

Look out for more titles in the Red Storybooks series:

Dinosaur Robbers by Jeremy Strong

Tyrannosaurus and Triceratops may look real, but they're actually two robotic dinosaurs invented by Max's dad. However, Buster and Binbag's beady eyes spy the dinosaurs and decide they'll come in handy for a spot of burglary....

Aliens in School by Jeremy Strong

On the day of Max's fancy dress party, the school is invaded by aliens intent on gobbling up all the party food, especially the jelly. Max must do something, but what?.

Magic Sponge by Michael Coleman

Is Barry Biggs ever going to get on the school football team? It's not much fun always standing on the touchline with Mr Simkin's bucket of water and sponges. But then Barry discovers Captain Tripp's magic sponge and thinks his big chance to be a star has come at last...

Thomas and the Tinners by Jill Paton Walsh

Thomas works in the tin mine where he meets some fairy miners who cause him a great deal of trouble – but then bring him good fortune. WINNER OF THE SMARTIES PRIZE.

Storybooks are available from your local bookshop, or can be ordered direct from the publishers. For more information about Storybooks, write to: *The Sales Department, Macdonald Young Books, 61 Western Road, Hove, East Sussex BN3 1JD.*